St. Helena Library

The Littles

Go Around the World

ISBN 0-439-20300-7

12 11 10 9 8 7 6 5 4 3 2 1   0 1 2 3 4 5 6/0

Printed in the U.S.A.
First Scholastic printing, November 2000

ER

Adapted by **Teddy Slater**
from ***THE LITTLES GO TO SCHOOL***
by **John Peterson**
Illustrated by **Jacqueline Rogers**

SCHOLASTIC INC.
New York Toronto London Auckland Sydney
Mexico City New Delhi Hong Kong

A whole lot of Littles

lived in the walls of

Mr. and Mrs. Bigg's house.

But they were so small,

the Biggs never

even noticed them.

The Littles only came out
of the walls when
the Biggs weren't around.

Mr. and Mrs. Little

spent lots of time

in the Biggs' kitchen.

So did Granny and Uncle Pete.

Cousin Dinky Little used the Biggs' roof as a landing strip for his glider plane.

And Tom and Lucy Little

often played in young

Henry Bigg's room.

Henry had lots of
toys and games.
But best of all,
he had two pet gerbils.

The gerbils were very small,

with nice long tails

— just like the Littles'.

One day Tom and Lucy were
playing in the gerbils' cage.
Suddenly they heard
Bigg loud footsteps!

Quick as a wink, they hid
under a pile of wood chips.
A Bigg hand picked up
the cage and carried it
out of the house.

13

A car door slammed.

An engine roared.

Mrs. Bigg drove off

with the cage,

the gerbils...

and two scared

Little children.

She drove all the way

to Henry's school.

"I've brought Henry's gerbils
for a visit," she told the class.
"You may keep them
for a week."

"Yay!" everyone cheered —
everyone except Tom and Lucy.
"Uh-oh!" they groaned
as Mrs. Bigg waved good-bye
and left.

"We have to get out
of here," Tom whispered.

"But how?" Lucy asked.

"The whole class is looking.
They'll see us if we move."

"Shh!" Tom hissed.

"I have an idea.

Watch me —

and get ready to run."

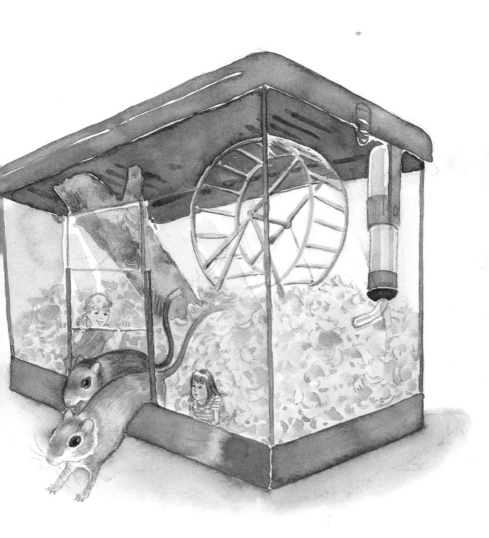

"Eek!" a girl yelled.

"The gerbils are loose!"

Everyone turned to watch

the animals dash across

the floor — everyone except Tom and Lucy.

They raced out the door,

down the hall, and into

an empty classroom.

Lucy pointed to a huge ball.

"What is that?" she asked.

"It's a globe," Tom said.

"A map of the whole Earth."

"Where is America?"

Lucy asked.

"You can't see it

from here," Tom said.

"You have to climb on top."

Lucy pulled herself all the

way up to the North Pole.

"Look at me!" she cried.

"I'm on top of the world."

Tom slowly spun the globe.
Lucy hopped onto Iceland,
jumped over Greenland, and
skipped across Canada.

Before long, she was
back where she started.
"Wow!" Lucy yelled.
"I just walked all
around the world!"

"Come on down," Tom said.

"Mom and Dad will be worried.

We should go now."

"But how?" Lucy said.

"We must be at least
a mile away from home."
Now, a mile may not
sound very far to you.
But Little legs are short.
One mile might just as well
be a million.

"There must be a way,"

Tom said....

...And sure enough, there was!

"How did you find us?"
Tom asked Cousin Dinky
as they flew home.
"I saw Mrs. Bigg drive off
with you," Dinky said.
"So I followed her car."

"We Littles have to stick together," Dinky said. "It's a great big world down there."